For Chet, Jessie, Kathy, and David too!
— R.H.H.

To Evan, for all his help.
— N.H.

Text copyright © 2005 by Bee Productions, Inc.
Illustrations copyright © 2005 by Nicole Hollander

Little, Brown and Company

Time Warner Book Group
1271 Avenue of the Americas, New York, NY 10020
Visit our Web site at www.lb-kids.com

First Edition: November 2005

Library of Congress Cataloging-in-Publication Data
Harris, Robie H.
 I LOVE messes! / Robie H. Harris ; illustrated by Nicole Hollander. — 1st ed.
   p. cm. — (Just being me)
 Summary: A little girl makes a huge mess playing in the kitchen. Includes brief notes about how children explore
their environment.
 ISBN 0-316-10946-0
 [1. Cleanliness — Fiction. 2. Orderliness — Fiction.] I. Hollander, Nicole, ill. II. Title. III. Series: Harris, Robie H. Just
being me.
PZ7.H2436Iabcd 2005 [E] — dc22
                                                                                                      2004025101

10 9 8 7 6 5 4 3 2 1

IM

Printed in China

The illustrations for this book were done in pen and ink. Color was added using Adobe Photoshop.
The text was set in Providence and Sylvia (designed by Nicole Hollander and Tom Greensfelder),
and the display type is Drunk Cyrillic.

just being
me

I LOVE LOVE Messes!

By Robie H. Harris

Illustrated by Nicole Hollander

LITTLE, BROWN AND COMPANY

New York ～ Boston

I love red! It's my very most favorite color.
Last night, I drew a big red circle—
so big it went right off the paper and onto the table.

ARF!

Daddy began to wipe the big red circle off the table.
Then he tried to wipe the big red dots
off my hands and face.
"NO!" I cried.

Daddy gave me strawberry yogurt.
I took a bite of my yogurt
and turned the cup upside down.
And I drew circles in the smooth pink yogurt—
with my thumbs.

Daddy opened the refrigerator.
"How about a carrot?" he asked.
"A carrot's NOT messy!" I said.

The doorbell rang.
Daddy handed me a carrot
and ran to answer the door.
"I'll be right back!" he said.

I peered into the refrigerator and touched an egg.

Then I touched every egg.

They felt cold and smooth.

I picked up one egg and dropped it!
And I watched it ooze all along the floor.

Then I dumped out some milk, some catsup, and some mustard too.

And I stepped into the egg, the milk, the catsup, and the mustard—and began to dance.

ARF!
ARF!

I twirled around and around in circles
in the cold, wet, slippery, mushy mess and sang,

MUSHY!
MESSY!

Our dog walked right through the mess.
Soon, her paw prints were all over the floor.

Then Daddy came back.
"This is fun!" I hollered.
"This is NOT fun!" said Daddy.
"You made a great big mess!
And it has to be cleaned up—now!"

SPLASH!

SPLASH!

"OKAY!" I cried. "I'm SORRY!"
"I know you are," said Daddy.

And we all cleaned up the

BIG,

THANKS FOR
HELPING,
Daddy.

At bath time, Daddy and I washed the strawberry yogurt out of my hair.

We washed the eggs, milk, mustard, and catsup off
my feet, and the bright red dots off my hands.
But Daddy left the red dots on my face.
"I kind of like them," he said.

At bedtime, Daddy whispered,
"No more messes! Okay?"
"No more messes," I whispered.
Soon, I had the best dream!

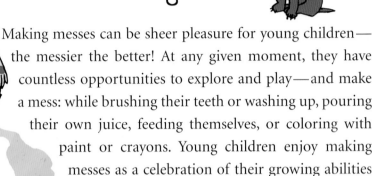

What's Going On?

Making messes can be sheer pleasure for young children—
the messier the better! At any given moment, they have
countless opportunities to explore and play—and make
a mess: while brushing their teeth or washing up, pouring
their own juice, feeding themselves, or coloring with
paint or crayons. Young children enjoy making
messes as a celebration of their growing abilities
to do more and more all by themselves.

The playful imagination of the young girl in this story is in full
swing as she gleefully mixes together colors and textures. But
what is pleasurable to a young child can pose conflicting feelings
for a parent. When the father in this story discovers the mess his
daughter has made, he is understandably exasperated. At the
same time, he realizes how much fun and how fascinating this
playing has been for his daughter, and that she was not trying to
do something naughty. He kindly and firmly lets her know that
purposely spilling food on the floor is not acceptable, and that
messes are not always fun for everyone and have to be cleaned
up. By cleaning up the mess with his daughter, and letting her